For Dr Jon

Vikings in the Supermarket
is a
DAVID FICKLING BOOK

First published in Great Britain in 2015 by
David Fickling Books,
31 Beaumont Street,
Oxford, OX1 2NP

Text and Illustrations © Nick Sharratt, 2015

978-1-910200-35-3

1 3 5 7 9 10 8 6 4 2

David Fickling Books supports the Forest Stewardship Council® (FSC®),
the leading international forest certification organisation.
All our titles that are printed on Greenpeace-approved FSC-certified paper carry the FSC logo.

MIX
Paper from
responsible sources
FSC® C104723

DAVID FICKLING BOOKS Reg. No. 8340307

A CIP catalogue record for this book is available from the British Library.

Printed and bound in China.

The tartan patterns in this book were created using
www.tartanmaker.com

Vikings
in the
Supermarket

Nick Sharratt

David Fickling Books

Vikings in the Supermarket

Six Vikings went shopping, they ran round the store,
'We need horns for our helmets,' they said.
But the store didn't sell helmet horns any more,
So they bought a few groceries instead.

Burt bought bananas.

Cora bought carrots.

Charlie bought cheeses.

Selwin bought sausages.

Ida bought ice-cream cones.

And Quentin bought croissants!

Six Vikings queued up and they paid at the till.
Then they rode home as pleased as can be.
Their helmets looked splendid, and added to that
There were lots of nice things left for tea!

The Mermaid and the Shoe

What would a mermaid do with a shoe?

She could see if it would float
Like a little sailing boat.

She could use it as a box
For her favourite shells and rocks.

It would make a comfy bed
For her pet crab, Winifred.

It might be just the thing
For growing seaweed in.

What a great home it could be
For a seahorse family!

How about a special dish
For feeding baby fish?

If she gave Sean Shark the shoe
It would make a tasty chew.

She could wear it as a hat.
No, she wouldn't fancy that.

Here's what a mermaid did with a shoe:

She pulled the lace out bit by bit
And strung a string of pearls on it.

A Tartan Tale

In bonny MacScotland,
High on a MacMountain,
With views of the salty MacSea,
There is a MacFarm
And it's here that you'll find
Farmer Fergal MacFindlay MacFee . . .

With his Scotty MacDog

And his purry MacCat,

His MacBudgies
(One green and one blue),

His oinky MacPig

And his woolly
MacSheep

And his greedy
MacBillygoat too.

He keeps clucky MacHens,
Who lay lovely MacEggs,
They're delicious,
Please take it from me.

And his Highland MacCattle
Make special MacPancakes . . .

. . . but not ones you'd want for your tea!

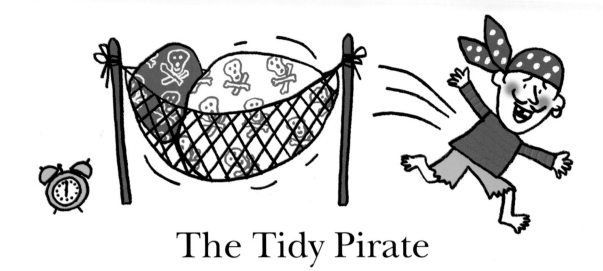

The Tidy Pirate

Early in the morning
Tidy Clyde jumps out of bed.
He gives a cheery 'Yo ho ho!'
There's pirating ahead!

But first he cooks his breakfast
And he feeds the parrot too,
Then there's vacuuming and dusting
And some polishing to do.

He opens up the treasure chest,
Gives everything a shine,
He puts the laundry through the wash
And hangs it on the line.

He gets on with the ironing,
The deck needs quite a scrub,
He cleans the porthole windows
And he rinses out the tub.

When everything is shipshape
Tidy Clyde is pleased as Punch.
He thinks about his afternoon
As he enjoys his lunch.

He'll chase a passing vessel
And he'll swiftly leap aboard.
If anybody wants a fight
He'll fiercely shake his sword!

He'll make off with a pile of gold,
Shiver me timbers! What fun!
But all of that must wait until . . .

. . . the washing-up is done!

Fangsalot

Vincent was a vampire bat,
The little rascal bit a cat.

The cat woke up, the cat mewed, 'Ow!'
It grew some fangs and bit a cow.

The cow grew fangs as well, of course,
It looked around and bit a horse.

The horse neighed, 'What a thing to do!'
And bit a passing kangaroo.

The kangaroo grew fangs, then pounced
And bit a hippo, unannounced.

The hippo let out quite a wail,
Grew fangs and bit a monkey's tail.

The monkey squealed, 'That isn't nice!'
And bit an ostrich, bit it twice.

The ostrich shrieked, 'I want my mum!'
And bit a panda on the bum.

The panda jumped and squealed, 'Why me?'
It grew some fangs and bit a tree.

And yes, the tree grew fangs as well,
It bit a snail right on its shell.

The snail slid off, it muttered, 'Drat!'
It grew some fangs and bit a hat.

The hat was cross, the hat yelled, 'Oi!'
It grew some fangs and bit a boy.

The boy just shrugged. He said, 'Tut tut,'
And bit into his jam doughnut.

Jam spurted out, it landed – splat!
On top of Vincent, vampire bat.

Sticky Vincent looked a sight,
And some might say it served him right!

Posh Paint

King Sid said, 'Crumbly Castle
Is a really dreary grey.
It is frightfully dull to look at
And it cannot stay this way!'

'It is time the place was painted
And I say let's paint it red.'
'Oh no!' exclaimed Queen Emily,
'It should be green instead.'

'Orange!' shouted Princess Charlotte.

'Yellow!' yelled Prince Hugh.

'Paint it black!' roared Princess Maud.

Prince Bernard bellowed, 'Blue!'

Princess Holly hollered, 'White!'

Prince Peter piped up, 'Pink!'

And the baby gurgled, 'Purple, please!'
(At least that's what they think.)

So they hummed and ha-ed and ha-ed and hummed
And they put their heads together . . .

Now dull grey Crumbly Castle
is the funkiest fortress ever!